Christmas on Georgian Bay

⚓

Published by Shore Girl Publications, Orillia, Ontario, Canada

First Printed Edition

Editor: Murray A. Cayley
Design, Layout and
Digital Production: Paul E. Dumais

Thank you:
Midland Free Press
Clement Clarke Moore
Todd L. Dumais

ISBN 978-0-9938113-0-2

For information: shoredoggeobay@gmail.com

You can always find us through the kind folks at the Huronia Museum, Midland, Ontario

B. G. Rourke Grew up on Georgian Bay and is the Author of the Book The Sea Cadet Years on Georgian Bay

Frances Hayter is a Watercolour Artist, Illustrator and Classical Pianist

Dedicated
to the
People and Animals
Up the Shore

North American Great Lakes

Lake Superior

Lake Michigan

Lake Huron

Georgian Bay

Lake Simcoe

Lake Ontario

Lake Erie

Drawn by an Elf on a Sky Trip to Map the Great Waters of the World

An Up the Shore Adventure

⚓

It was Christmas Eve on Georgian Bay. A wind was blowing snow across the ice and along the rocky shores of Blueberry Island where Shoredog lived with his friends Dusty the horse, Snowball, a white cat, his shore family, Frank, Nita and their children Joe, Holly and Goldie.

This was a time before electricity and telephones up the shore, time when travel was by horse and homemade sleighs, time when animals and people took care of each other.

Blueberry Island Point

⚓

Another friend, Grey Owl, lived in a tree next to the house. A herd of deer, who made their home on nearby Beausoleil Island, was their closest neighbour. Sometimes they wandered across the ice to visit and munch on the branches of cedar trees growing in the marsh.

Shoredog and Dusty lived in a barn just a short walk from Frank and Nita's house, but Shoredog was always welcome in the family home.

He trotted over to their house now and scratched at the door.

Grey Owl in Great White Pine

"There you are old boy." Nita said with affection as she opened the door. "Come in by the fire, it's Christmas Eve and the children are very excited."

Shoredog looked around at the decorations in the living room; a tree with a star on top shimmered with tinsel and shiny, coloured balls. Candles flickered on the dining room table.

"Very nice," Shoredog woofed to himself.

WOOF

Shoredog born in Newfoundland

An Up the Shore Adventure 7

A fire was blazing in the fireplace and three of Frank's grey wool work socks hung from the mantel with Joe written on one and Goldie and Holly written on the other two.

Shoredog sniffed the air and smelled freshly baked cakes and cookies. Some of the cookies were set out on a plate, a snack for Santa.

⚓

The children, sitting by the fire, were listening to their father play Christmas carols on his old fiddle.

"Hi Shoredog," greeted Joe. "Santa is coming tonight and I've asked for a new sled."

"He's bringing me a new doll," Holly said as she patted Shoredog's head.

"I want a tea set," chimed in Goldie, "a porcelain tea pot with cups and saucers."

"Woof," answered Shoredog wagging his tail.

Shoredog lay contentedly by the fire with his family, listening to the music, thumping his tail when the children clapped, calling for "more music Daddy." But soon, it was bedtime.

"Good-night Shoredog," they said as they gave the happy dog a hug on their way to bed with Mom and Dad following to tuck them in.

Frank's Old Fiddle
Given to him by his Father

⚓

TAP! TAP!

A sharp tap-tap at the window startled Shoredog. He looked up and saw Grey Owl motioning with his wing for him to go outside.

Shoredog heaved his black furry body up from the floor woofing until Frank came to open the door.

"Go and keep Dusty company in the barn." Frank said. "We'll see you in the morning. Merry Christmas Shoredog."

Grey Owl was perched in the great white Pine just outside the door.

Grey Owl Delivers a Message

"What's the matter, Grey Owl?" Shoredog asked. "You look worried."

Grey Owl hooted excitedly. "I just got a message from Great White Owl that Santa needs you to take over the up the shore route this year. I told him you and Dusty could do it. Meet Santa at the Midland town dock at midnight. They will give you a list of the children and the toys they asked the Elves to make. I'll let Great White Owl know you will be there."

With that Grey Owl disappeared into the night leaving Shoredog staring after him.

"OH MY GOSH!" Woofed a stunned Shoredog as he turned and ran towards the barn.

⚓

Woof! Woof! Woof! Oh My Gosh! Woof!

"Dusty," Shoredog woofed breathlessly, skidding to a stop, "you won't believe what we have to do tonight!"

"What's happened? Is our shore family OK!?" Dusty asked his voice rising in alarm.

"Nothing like that," woofed Shoredog, "but we have a big job ahead of us and we don't have much time."

"A BIG JOB!" He added dramatically.

When Shoredog finished telling Dusty about Santa's request for help, they stood staring at each other in shocked silence. Finally, Dusty took a bite of hay from the manger and started to pace around the barn. Shoredog sat and watched and thought and thought.

"It's impossible for us to do this ourselves Dusty." Woofed Shoredog. "We have to get Frank to help us. Wait here and get ready to go."

Neigh neigh. Whinny, whinny, whinny Neigh? Whinny. Neigh, neigh. Oh NEIGH!

Woof! Woof? Woof, woof, woof. Bow WoW!

Shoredog and Dusty discuss how to let Frank know Santa needs them.

Shoredog ran out the barn door and, at the house he BARKED and BARKED until Nita opened the door. "Shoredog!" She scolded, "Stop your BARKING, the children are sleeping!"

Shoredog lowered his bark as he ran to Frank and pulled at his sleeve. Several times he ran back and forth between the door and Frank tugging on his sleeve, woofing for him to follow. WOOF! WOOF! WOOF! WOOF!

"I think he wants me to follow him," Frank told Nita. "I'll go out with him for a while."

Once outside Shoredog tugged Frank's coat and pulled him towards the barn.

"OK boy," Frank said, "lead the way."

Bark Bark.
Woof Woof.
Woof Bark Bark
Bow WOW!

⚓

Shoredog ran back to the barn and Frank found him there pulling at Dusty's harness hanging on the wall.

Frank was puzzled. "What is going on?" he asked.

Shoredog ran between the harness, Dusty and the sleigh until Dusty trotted out of the barn to the sleigh and stood looking at Frank.

"What in blazes?!" Frank exclaimed. "You want to be hitched to the sleigh? Something is very odd with you two tonight."

Dusty Stood in Front of the Sleigh Trying to Help Frank Understand

⚓

Just then Nita hurried into the barn with a note in her hand.

"Look Frank," she said excitedly. "This note dropped from Grey Owl's perch in the great white Pine. It says Shoredog and Dusty are to take the sleigh and meet Santa and his reindeer at the Midland town dock at midnight. Santa needs them to make his Christmas deliveries to all the children up the shore."

"Frank," she said in a grave voice, "you must go, Santa needs your help!"

"Well, I'll be darned," he said in wonder as he took the harness off the wall, put it on Dusty and hitched him to the sleigh.

They put boards around the flat sleigh to make a box, loaded hay for Dusty to eat and food for Shoredog. As Shoredog jumped aboard, Nita put a hamper with hot cocoa and homemade bread and jam for Frank under the seat.

Great White Owl's Note in Owl Words

(Human Translation)
IMPORTANT NOTE FROM GREAT WHITE OWL

Dear Grey Owl:
Please let Shoredog and Dusty know that they have to find a way to get Frank to understand that he <u>must</u> come with them in his sleigh to the Midland town dock and be there by midnight. Santa needs them to deliver all the Christmas presents for the up the shore children tonight.

Please hurry!

Your friend
Great White Owl

"This might be a wild goose chase," Frank said, as he kissed Nita good-bye, "but we can't risk letting Santa and the shore children down at Christmas."

"Giddy up Dusty!" He shouted and they headed off the island out onto the ice. A big, full moon shone down lighting their way and stars sparkled like diamonds in the sky. Dusty's hoofs thundered across the snowy ice as he sped over Smooth Rock, past Brébeuf Lighthouse and along the shore of Beausoleil. As they reached the point of Beausoleil where it jutted into the Gap, Frank called, "Whoa, Dusty. Slow down boy. Sometimes the ice out from this point is not very safe. I'll walk ahead and test it before I take you and Shoredog out on it."

Dusty slowed and then stopped. He snorted and whinnied and shook his head, calming himself after the excitement of the fast run down the Bay.

Brébeuf Lighthouse on small
island offshore Beausoleil Island

⚓

Frank quickly jumped out of the sleigh, taking with him a heavy iron pole used for testing the ice. Shoredog watched him head out into the dark. Soon he heard THUMP, THUMP, THUMP as Frank plunged the iron pole into the ice and listened to the sound. A deep, heavy thump meant the ice was thick and safe. Soon, he was running back towards them.

"It's OK boys," Frank told them. "Run like the wind Dusty. It's almost midnight and we can't be late."

"Heigh Ho Dusty!" Woofed Shoredog.

Beausoleil Island Point

⚓

As they rounded Midland Point Shoredog could see Santa's red sleigh in the distance.

"Wow, Bow WOW!" Shoredog woofed to himself with awe. A glow surrounded the waiting group and bells jingled softly as the reindeer turned to watch them approach.

Shoredog shook himself with his happy dogness and grinned from ear to ear.

"There's Dasher and Dancer, Prancer and Vixen," he woofed, "and there's Comet standing near Cupid and, WOW, Donner and Blitzen are looking right at us."
Then Shoredog gasped in surprise as a pink glow moved from behind the reindeer into view.

Dasher, Dancer and Prancer, There's Vixen, Comet and Cupid. WoW! There's Donner and Blitzen!

⚓

He stared in awe realizing the pink glow was shimmering around his childhood "up the shore" friend Reine. She was a White-tailed deer who grew up on nearby Beausoleil Island. Shoredog remembered when Reine was a little girl deer she told anyone who would listen that she was destined to help Santa when she grew up because her name was Reine Deer. Lately there had been rumours up the shore that Santa was training a new recruit this year. "And here she is," thought Shoredog. "BUT, Reine is LEADING Santa and his reindeer team!" He said to himself with amazement, shaking his furry body to help stay calm.

Reine Deer

As Frank guided Dusty alongside Santa's sleigh Santa Ho Ho Hoed a greeting to them.

"Dusty," Santa said, "let my Elves wipe you down after the fast, long run you've had. You don't want to get cold, you still have a long way to go tonight."

"Santa," Frank asked, "how can we possibly help you? The distance is great and time is very short before all the children up the shore will be up searching for their gifts under the tree."

"As you can see," Santa said as he motioned towards the white tailed deer, "I have a new team leader this year guiding us through the night. We have many extra children who believe in Christmas now. We didn't get notice of this until just before we started our journey. We don't have any spare minutes for emergencies. Reine mentioned that you, Shoredog and Dusty know this area better than anyone and you believe in the magic of Christmas."

How can we help you Santa?

"Reine" Santa called, beckoning to the white tailed deer, "come and say hello to your friends."

As Reine trotted over, the pink glow shimmered around her. Frank gave her a big hug and a pat on the back. Shoredog woofed and wagged his tail in admiration and Dusty neighed a "good to see you again friend."

Santa turned back to Frank with a twinkle in his eyes and explained:

"Christmas is a magical time. After I sprinkle some magic dust on Dusty's hoofs, Reine is going to teach him to fly." "And," he added to the astonished trio, "I have magic dust for you Frank to put on the side of your nose so you can get down the chimneys."

Santa and His Magic Dust

Turning to Shoredog he told him, "I will sprinkle magic night vision dust on your eyes so that you can show them the way in the dark. But you must all work together and trust in the magic of Christmas," he added solemnly. "And," he added, "there is other special magic that you know and must remember." He leaned closer and whispered something to them.

Then he reached into his red and gold sleigh and brought out a little golden pot.

"Are you ready?" Santa asked.

"Yes Santa," Frank said for them. "We are ready."

Santa filled his hand from the golden pot and threw the magic dust over Frank, Dusty and Shoredog. Dusty's feet began to glow and Shoredog's eyes to shine. With a sneeze and a snuffle, Frank felt his nose tingling and knew they were ready to begin.

"You and Shoredog must hang on tight," Santa said to Frank, "because only Dusty can fly. Now prepare yourselves and Reine will give Dusty some flying lessons. But remember, the magic dust will wear off at daybreak, you must be home by then."

⚓

Shoredog's Eyes Began to Shine and Dusty's Hoofs
Began to Glow

Frank and Shoredog got onto their sleigh where <u>Elves</u> had been busy filling it full of dolls and sleds, skates and skis, books and trains, candy, puzzles and everything nice.

"Dusty," Reine said. "you must trust the magic dust. Do not be afraid. Run in the sky as you run on the ground, it helps keep your balance. Stay on a straight course and don't turn sharply or the sleigh will start to swing back and forth and could spin you out of control. So, be calm and careful. You can trust my advice," she added with a happy grin, "I've had a lot of good reindeer teachers."

Reine stood next to Dusty. "We will do a couple of trial runs, taking off and landing. Do exactly what I do. Lets go!" She shouted.

(These Elves are Grampa and Granny Elves who worked for Santa for a long, long time and now live near Santa's vacation home in Muskoka, just north of Midland. Great White Owl asked them to come down to help with transferring the Christmas parcels to Frank's sleigh and anything else that was needed in this emergency.)

⚓

You Must Trust the Magic Dust Reine told Dusty

Off they went across the snow. Reine seemed to just lift off the ice and called for Dusty to do the same. Dusty got his speed up and pulled his front hoofs off the ice and pushed himself into the air. Frank guided him with long leather straps attached to the face harness, following Reine in a slow circle and then down to land on the ice. Their sleigh veered and bumped a little but came to a halt next to Santa's.

They practiced one more time, lifting off the ice, climbing into the sky and circling to land again.

"Well done." Santa Ho, Ho, Hoed. "You are ready, my friends. You have the list of names. You know where they live. Be sure to be home before day break. Now I must be on my way. Thank you for your help on this very important night," he called as Reine led the reindeer lifting into the air.

Frank, Shoredog and Dusty watched them climb into the sky and circle towards Penetanguishene and Perkinsfield and could hear: "On Dasher, on Dancer, on Prancer and Vixen. On Comet on Cupid, on Donner and Blitzen. Merry Christmas my friends, trust in the magic of Christmas."

They Practiced Taking off and Landing in Midland
Harbour

"OK Dusty," Frank said, "it's time for us to climb into the sky too. Shoredog, you show us the way with your night vision. Our first stop is Cognashene. There are three families there. Giddy up Dusty. Yee Haw!" Frank shouted.

Dusty pulled on the heavy sleigh and started to run, faster and faster and leapt into the air.

"I'm flying! I'm flying!" Whinnied Dusty.

In his enthusiasm he swerved a little too much and heard Frank give a shout. He looked back and Shoredog was hanging on to one of the runners for dear life. Dusty slowed some and Frank bent over the edge and grabbed Shoredog's paw. The sleigh slithered from side to side as Shoredog hooked his back paws on the runner and pushed himself back into the sleigh.

"Be careful." Frank called to Dusty "We almost lost Shoredog."

"Woof, woof, woof." Woofed Shoredog with a little shiver.

This way To Iron City, Sans Souci
Woods Bay, Moon River and Beyond

Cognashene Point Here
Muskoka is Eastwards

Hope Island and
Lighthouse

Blueberry Island

Smooth Island

Beausoleil
Island

Giant's Tomb

Beckwith Island

Brébeuf
Lighthouse

Sawlog Bay

Christian Island

Pinery Point

Hallen's .Rock

Thunder Bay

Present .Island

To the East Are Port McNicol and
Victoria Harbour

Lafontaine   Perkinsfield

Penetanguishene

Midland

A Not So Accurate Sleigh-in-the-Sky View Map of
Santa's Up the Shore Route

Dusty pulled the sleigh higher and higher into the sky through the millions of years of starshine glimmering down upon them. Two green beams of light shone from Shoredog's eyes lighting the way below. Off to the east were the ships Assiniboia and Keewatin at their winter birth in Port McNicol. To the west, Giant's Tomb lay in dark outline against the white frozen Bay. They flew over Beausoleil, Kindersley and Whalens, As they approached Cognashene, Shoredog shone his magic night vision light on the first of the houses. Dusty slowly circled, getting lower and lower in the sky. He had to be careful landing on the roof; too heavy a drop and they might fall through, too fast and he might run right off the roof and nose dive into the ground.

"Easy Dusty." Frank said in a quiet voice so the children in the house below wouldn't hear. He pulled gently on the reins. "Slow down a little more." He coaxed. "You're doing just fine."

The roof was under them now and Dusty dropped lightly and brought the sleigh gently down behind him.

"Wow!" Dusty whinnied quietly, smiling to himself. "I'm liking this!"

⚓

The Moon Shone Down as they passed through Millions of Years of Starshine

At the next two Cognashene homes they left more skis, sleds, two dolls, books, a telescope, toy trucks and all that was wished for. Dusty took a bite of hay while Frank went down the chimney and Shoredog chewed on one of his special doggie treats. "You have to keep your energy up." Frank told them.

Frank popped out of the chimney and got into the sleigh. Dusty made a running leap off the roof and climbed high into the sky this time. Shoredog turned his gaze towards the horizon and saw the dark shape of Hope Island Lighthouse and Christian Island out past Giant's Tomb.

They flew over Sans Souci and circled the caretaker's house at Iron City. There was a strong west wind and Dusty had to make a couple of passes, but, with a bump and a thump, they landed safely on the roof. A cold wind ruffled Dusty's mane and Shoredog's fur. A coyote was yip-yipping in the forest and the ice boomed as it formed in the cold Georgian Bay.

⚓

With a Bump and a Thump They landed safely

Frank jumped out of the sleigh, checked his list twice and unloaded a doll, skates, a train set, a pair of skis and many other things the children in the house below were dreaming of.

He walked to the chimney and, putting his finger to the side of his nose, down the chimney he went. It was so quick he didn't even feel the couple of times he bumped his head. Inside he placed the toys around the tree, ate the cookies on the plate and was glad for the glass of milk to drink.

Cookies and Milk
on Blue Plate

Again, he put his finger to the side of his nose and up the chimney he rose.

Bringing Happiness on Christmas Morning

Back on the roof Frank said to them, "We're off to Woods Bay and Moon River. Show us the way Shoredog."

They climbed high over Captain Allen Straits and Moon Island startling a herd of deer bedded down for the night.

Now that Frank had some chimney experience he quickly popped down each of the chimneys of the four families in Woods Bay, leaving much happiness for the children to wake to in the morning. He banged his head going down a different type of chimney in Moon River but the homemade lemon pie set out for Santa helped him feel better.

As they leapt into the sky from the last roof in Moon River, Shoredog could see the children rush out of the house to stare up at them.

"Uh, oh." Woofed Shoredog.

"Ho, Ho, Ho," Frank shouted in his best deep Santa's voice.

"Merry Christmas, Merry Christmas to one and all!"

Ho Ho Ho
Merry Christmas,
Merry Christmas
to one and all.

⚓

"Now, my friends," he said to Dusty and Shoredog, "we must hurry. We have two more houses before we reach home and it's almost daybreak."

Dusty climbed higher and higher and ran faster and faster. Shoredog hung on and shone his light for Dusty to follow.

"We're coming up to the Freddy Channel soon." Frank called. "Our next stop is just over there," he added pointing towards a house nestled among the trees and rocks.

Dusty made a perfect landing. Frank gathered up all the presents on the list and down the chimney he went. It didn't take very long and once more they were in the air, heading for the Musquash. It was their last house before home and none too soon. Daybreak was almost upon them. They circled the house and came in just over the tree tops, landing with a jingle of the harness.

Down the chimney Frank went, placing the dolls, trucks, sleds and all the other gifts from the list under the tree. In the kitchen, next to the homemade oatmeal cookies and a glass of milk, was a note.

Oh Christmas Tree

With not a moment to spare he put the cookies and note in his pocket, drank half the milk and went to the chimney, put his finger on the side of his nose and up the chimney he rose. He would read the note when he got home.

As he ran to the sleigh the note fell from his pocket and Shoredog shone his eyes on it. Frank stooped to pick it up and read:

Dear Santa:
I love you. I am riting for a favor from you. I have a frend who is afriad to trust in the magic of Christmas. Culd you rite her a note and leeve it here. and, if you have an extra doll culd you leeve it for her. I know she reely wants one. Her name is Jennifer.
love
Carolyn
P.S. I helped my mommy make the cookies.
I love all the reindeer too.

"Oh Shoredog, what am I going to do?" Frank asked in dismay. "I don't think we have extra toys and dawn is about to break. We've got to hurry or we will lose our magic dust power before we get home."

Shoredog woofed soothingly to Frank as he searched the sleigh. There were no extra toys. The only doll in the sleigh was for Holly.

Frank thought for a moment. Then he said to Shoredog and Dusty, "Santa told us to trust in the magic of Christmas." "And," he added, "remember Santa whispered special advice reminding us that the most powerful magic is kindness. I have an idea. If it doesn't work, I will have to leave Holly's doll for Jennifer. Holly has a kind heart. I know she will understand if Santa leaves her a note."

Shoredog and Dusty watched Frank, curious to see what he would do.

⚓

With a small knife from his pocket, Frank scraped a little magic flying dust from Dusty's hoofs onto the note. Next he asked Shoredog to blink and a little magic dust for night vision fell onto the piece of paper. He tapped the side of his nose and some magic chimney dust sprinkled onto the others. He mixed the three together, walked over to the doll in the sleigh and threw the dust over her.

With a tinkling sound, a shimmery light rose from the sleigh. Shoredog looked in and woofed with anticipation. And there, to Frank's surprise, was a beautiful new doll with long hair, beautiful green eyes and a long golden dress.

Dusty and Shoredog Watching a Shimmery Light

With no time to waste, Frank scratched out a note in the best Santa writing he could.

Dear Jennifer:
I trust in the magic of Christmas,
the magic of friends and the magic of you.
love
Santa and friends.
P.S. Love to Carolyn too.

When he finished writing he put his finger at the side of his nose and down the chimney he went. He placed the doll under the tree and the note next to the half cup of milk and, with his finger at the side of his nose, up the chimney he rose.

Down the Chimney He Goes

Shoredog woofed as he looked towards the pale horizon.

"We have little time my friends," Frank said as he jumped into the sleigh, "we've got to fly like the wind. Not too high Dusty in case we have to land in a hurry."

Off they flew, skimming the ice and rocks. Dusty ran faster and faster making the bells on his harness jingle louder and louder. They scared a flock of ducks and geese swimming in a stretch of open water. They quacked and honked and flapped their wings, rushing this way and that as the strange thing flew over them. QUACK! QUACK! HONK! HONK! QUAACK!!

"Run Dusty, run." called Frank. "We have only a few minutes to get home."

Dusty was running faster than the wind. Behind him the sleigh swung to and fro. Shoredog's fur blew straight back and Frank laughed out loud with the happiness of it all.

Finally, Blueberry Island was in sight.

QUACK, QUACK!! Let's get out of here!

Quacky! Quacky! I want my Mommy!

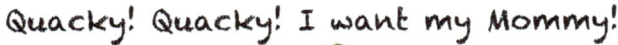

QUACK! QUACK! QUAAACK!!! DIVE! DIVE! DIVE!

QUACK! QUACK!!! The Sky is falling!

QUACK, QUACK! Is that you Dusty? WHAT are you doing up THERE?!!

"Whoa, slow down Dusty. Good boy. Let's land behind the house in case any of the children are up."

Just as they were about to touch down, the magic dust in Dusty's hoofs left him and he thump, bumped and stumbled to a stop.

"Good boy, Dusty. Good boy." Frank exclaimed as he jumped off the sleigh and patted the horse's neck.

"You're a good boy too, Shoredog," Frank told him as he hugged the black dog.

Home Sweet Home

⚓

Nita ran out to greet them.

"Quickly," Frank said, as he gave her a kiss hello, "let's get Santa's presents into the house. I'll put them around the tree while you fill the stockings. I'll tell you our story when we get everyone settled."

With the last of Santa's work done and Joe's sled, Holly's doll and Goldie's Tea set under the tree, Frank unhitched Dusty and called Shoredog. Slowly the three friends walked towards the barn, exhausted but happy.

Frank gave his two companions fresh water and food; dried Dusty and fluffed Shoredog's pillow. As he was leaving the barn he quietly said to them: "We were a good team my friends.

Merry Christmas Dusty. Merry Christmas Shoredog."

MERRY CHRISTMAS DEAR FRIENDS

⚓

www.ingramcontent.com/pod-product-compliance
Lightning Source LLC
Chambersburg PA
CBHW041536240626

47164CB00002B/30